PAPI JOINS THE BAND

By Tracey West
Illustrated by Jay Johnson

ISBN 0-439-78959-1
© 2006 Scholastic Entertainment Inc.

12 11 10 9 8 7 6 5 4 3 2 1   6 7 8 9 10/0
Printed in the U.S.A.
First printing, March 2006

SCHOLASTIC INC.

New York   Toronto   London   Auckland   Sydney
Mexico City   New Delhi   Hong Kong   Buenos Aires

Miguel, Theo, and Andy stood on the school cafeteria line.

They were excited—but not about lunch.

They were trying to come up with an act for the Community Center Talent Show.

"I know!" Miguel said. "We can start a band!"

His friends liked the idea.

Miguel's sister, Maya, overheard them.

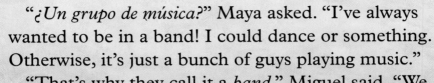

"*¿Un grupo de música?*" Maya asked. "I've always wanted to be in a band! I could dance or something. Otherwise, it's just a bunch of guys playing music."

"That's why they call it a *band*," Miguel said. "We are all about the music!"

Maya found Tito in the hallway. "Miguel doesn't want me in his band," she said sadly.

"Why not show him what he is missing?" Tito suggested.

Maya's eyes lit up, along with her hair bobbles. "*¡Eso es,* Tito! That's it!"

While Maya worked on her idea, the boys set up in Miguel's basement. Miguel sat behind his drums. Theo stood with his synthesizer. Andy got his turntables ready for action.

"The first thing we need is a name," Miguel said. "How about 'Miguel and the Backup Boys'?"

"I was thinking of 'The Andy Experience,'" Andy suggested.
"It should be something simple, like 'Theo'!" Theo said.
    Miguel frowned. "Maybe we should forget about the
name for now and just practice!"

After practice, Miguel talked to his parents.

"I think our band has a good chance of winning the contest," he said.

Mrs. Santos smiled. "You know, your father was in a band."

"Wow, that's so cool, Papi!" Miguel said. "Being in a band is a lot of work. You have to come up with a name, and a look, and get everyone to work together. . . ."

"Just remember, it's all about the music," Mr. Santos said. "Stay focused on the music, and everything will take care of itself."

Miguel took Papi's advice. When the boys practiced again, they focused on the music. Miguel struck up a beat with his drums. "Let's have a little keyboard action, Theo," he said.

Theo played a funky melody on his keyboard. It fit right in with Miguel's beat.

Andy started scratching records, adding rhythm to the sound.

The boys were in a groove when Papi walked in, carrying a conga drum.

"Miguel, I figured out what you were trying to tell me before," he said.

Miguel was confused. "What was I trying to tell you?"

Papi grinned. "I'm here to help you out with your band!"

Papi got right to work. He helped the boys come up with a name for the band: "The New Cats."

"That's great, Mr. Santos. Thanks!" Andy said.

"I can't wait for our next practice!" Mr. Santos said.

Miguel got nervous. "Next practice?" Did Papi think he was in the band?

Maya and Tito still wanted to be in Miguel's band.
They danced into the living room.

"Maya and Tito are in the house!"

Tito tried to break-dance. He spun around on his back.

Maya tripped over Tito. A vase flew up in the air, just as Paco flew in. The family parrot wanted to join the band, too.

"Paco's in the house!"

Plop! The vase fell on Paco's head.

Meanwhile, the boys kept practicing for the contest—and Mr. Santos kept coming.

"You can't have a band without a beat," he said. "You need rhythm!"

But Mr. Santos' ideas about rhythm were different.

He used maracas and the conga drum to add rhythm. He didn't understand why Andy scratched his records. He didn't get what a shout-out was, either.

"Don't shout during the song!" he said. "It interferes with the music."

Miguel tried to talk to his father.
"Maybe we should practice on our own," he said.
But Mr. Santos didn't get it. "It's no problem. I'm happy to help out a little more!"

Mr. Santos got more and more excited. He gave the boys matching suits to wear. He tried to teach them to dance. But the boys just tripped over each other.

Mr. Santos got carried away. He got a smoke machine and a disco ball. He made T-shirts and posters for the band.

He forgot his own advice: "*Stay focused on the music.*"

The boys were trying to figure out what to do when Maya and Tito rolled in.

"Maya, we don't need unicycles in our band!" Miguel cried.

"You need to read this flyer," Maya said. "Willie B. Chill is going to judge the talent contest!"

"Willie B. Chill is a hip-hop star," Miguel moaned. "We can't let him see us like this!"

Soon came the night of the talent show. The boys stood backstage, growing more and more nervous. The suits, the lights, the smoke—it just wasn't *them*.

"Miguel, we really like your dad," Andy said. "But . . ."
"We think it should just be the three of us tonight," Theo said.
Andy nodded. "You need to ask him to leave the band."

Miguel didn't want to hurt his father's feelings. But he knew his friends were right.

"Papi, when you joined the band, it was really cool," he said. "But it wasn't our own thing. Tonight we need to do this by ourselves."

Mr. Santos finally understood.

"This is your night," he said. "Trust yourself, and do it your own way."

Maya and Tito overheard. "Tonight, we'll do *our* own thing, too," Maya said.

Just then, Willie B. Chill walked up.

"Santiago Santos!" he cried. He hugged Miguel's dad.

Miguel could not believe it. "Papi, you know Willie B. Chill?"

"Sure," Papi said. "We used to be in a band together."

It was time for the show to begin.
Maya and Tito did a trampoline act.
Tito tripped, but that made the act even better.
Maya and Tito bounced up to the ceiling!
Maya grabbed a rope. They swung down and landed
onstage. Then they took a bow.
The crowd went wild!

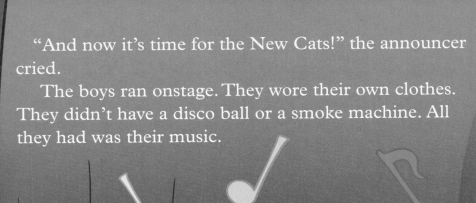

"And now it's time for the New Cats!" the announcer cried.

The boys ran onstage. They wore their own clothes. They didn't have a disco ball or a smoke machine. All they had was their music.

"New Cats in the house!" Miguel cried.
The boys rocked to their own beat.

When the contest was over, Willie B. Chill stood up.
"Second prize goes to the New Cats!" he announced.

The boys cheered.

"Your dad is one cool cat," Willie told Miguel. "You could learn a lot from him."

Miguel smiled. "I already did!"

Later that night, Maya and Miguel talked about the contest.

"Our band sounded great," Miguel said. "I'm glad we found our rhythm."

Maya smiled. "Aren't you forgetting something, Miguel?"

Miguel rolled his eyes. "Oh, yeah."

Maya grinned. "Tito and I won first prize!"

DO YOU REMEMBER?

CIRCLE The righT answer.

1. WhaT advice did Papi first give The boys?
a. STay focused on your cosTumes.
b. STay focused on The music.
c. STay focused on The disco ball.

2. Which insTrumenT did MigueL use To keep The beaT?
a. The drums
b. The keyboard
c. a guiTar

3. Why does Andy scraTch records on a TurnTable?
a. To add sound and rhyThm To The music
b. because he doesn'T Like records
c. To annoy Mr. SanTos